Juli, 1973.

Der lieben Evi –
Zum neunten! Geburtstag
mit vielen lieben Wünschen
von Stephanie und Ernest-Mark
Denham.

Norman Rockwell's
HOMETOWN

TOLD BY THOMAS ROCKWELL

Windmill Books / New York

Published by Windmill Books Inc.
An Intext Publisher
257 Park Ave. South
New York, New York
SBN 0-87807-008-7 Trade
SBN 0-87807-009-5 Library
Library of Congress Catalog Card Number: 78-130217

Norman Rockwell

CHOCOLATE CAKE

"Haw. Haw. Haw. Haw."

"Cut it out, Sam. I'm warning you."

"Jack's got a girl friend, Jack's got a girl friend. Haw. Haw. *Hey, Joe!*" yelled Sam.

Joe skidded his bike to a racing stop beside them.

"Guess who was carrying Lucy Thompson's books to school this morning?" crowed Sam.

"Who?" said Joe, examining the front tire of his bike.

"Look at him blush."

"You mean Jack?"

"Look at him."

"Naw! Jack? Jack, was it you?"

"Of course, it was him. He handed them back behind Howard's Store so no one would see him. Haw. Haw. I was hiding in the bushes by the fence."

"My mother made me," said Jack.

A screen door slammed. A girlish voice called, "Jack? Jack?"

"There," said Sam. "What'd I tell you?"

"Jack," said Lucy, coming to the gate. "The cake's ready."

Sam and Joe hung over the fence, razzing and catcalling Jack for "having tea, just you and me" on the porch with Lucy. Jack never gave them a glance, just carved out a second slice of chocolate-cake-dripping-icing...

Sam and Joe fell silent, watching him fork a crumbly hunk (Sam could almost taste it way out there at the gate) into his mouth... and carefully lick his fingers... and...

Joe gulped and looked sick and, turning, wheeled his bike off down the road. Sam started to yell, "Hey, Jack, give..." and then realized it was futile and slunk off home, suffering.

A DRAW

"We almost got him!" crowed Billy, standing in the kitchen door, dripping wet, pickerel weed in his hair.

"Billy! My clean floor!"

"We almost caught him, Mom! I slung into his hole up to the further end where it's deepest and Gramps figures he likes to feed in the mornings. And Gramps slung into the lower end because he said it was a day to make old bones feel spry again, and he figured Big Daddy might be moving. Then Gramps lit his pipe and I sucked a pebble and we waited. And it was so quiet, Mom, a mushrat came right up on the bank near me and gathered a mouthful of weeds and swam all the way across the still pool; I was almost going to sleep, my eyes closing, Mom, when WHAMMO! my float—the red float I got for Christmas? It looked like the pool had swallowed it! Gulp! The line sang in my reel, I was scrambling up, and all of a sudden my pole *jerked!*—he's taken all my line in about, I don't know, *six seconds!*—and I tumbled right into the pool, splash! but I hung on, thrashing in the shallows, till Gramps caught hold of my foot, and that must have snapped my line because all of a sudden I couldn't feel anything pulling anymore, and then SPLASH! even bigger than …I mean, you know…" Billy reddened. "I mean splash we didn't catch him after all," he finished lamely.

"Father," said Billy's mother. "Stop hiding behind the door."

Billy's grandfather looked around the door, his dripping pipe clamped upside down in his mouth.

"Well," said Billy's mother. "It looks to me as if you two not only didn't catch Big Daddy—it looks to me as if he caught you."

"Nope," said Billy's grandfather. "It was a draw. He didn't get us any further in than we got him out. It was a clean draw."

"Except that he took my hook and sinkers," said Billy.

SCROWWWWWWGH!

Ned didn't believe in ghosts. How could he believe in ghosts? He was seven and a half going on eight. Still, he realized no one had ever really *proved* there weren't any ghosts...even if everyone *knew* there weren't any. Ned scratched his head, standing in the pumpkin field.

So the thing was: he'd go along with Halloween, but he'd take precautions. He'd carve out a jack-o'-lantern to please his father, but he'd sleep under his bed. And he'd go out trick or treating, but he'd be home before real dark. Honk!

He jumped. Geese! Sounded just like a ghost.

So he went out that evening with Eddie and George, and they got fooling around, jumping out from behind bushes pretending to scare each other, and by the time Ned thought to look around him, there was nothing but darkness outside the bright pools under the streetlights and a dog howling over on Loft Street. Ned slogged on home.

Coming up Elm, he saw his jack-o'-lantern glimmering on the porch railing. He hoped...*Say!* It hadn't moved!?! Wobbled? How could a jack-o'-lantern?...just an old dead pumpk...*Say!* There it went again! Like it was trying to fly off the railing at him!

Ned stood still on the sidewalk, watching it. The house was dark behind it, but he could see light leaking from the kitchen window around back. He'd chance a dash to the front door. Otherwide he'd have to go through the bushes and dark along the side. *He grabbed his head! The pumpkin was taking off* RIGHT AT HIM!

He lit out around the house as the jack-o'-lantern toppled off the railing and rolled across the lawn toward the sidewalk, its candle guttering out.

Scrowwwwwwgh! His sister's cat leapt down from the porch railing and began to wash its face.

IDEAS

Mr. Springer and Tom had just finished taking inventory in the backroom, climbing on stepladders to take down dusty boxes, counting shoes, lanterns, baseball caps.

The bell on the front door tinkled. Mr. Springer went off to wait on the customer. Tom began to pile the boxes back up. Then he had an idea. He'd stack them…sure…wait till…Mr. Springer'd probably give him a raise.

By the time Mr. Springer returned, Tom had stacked all the boxes, neatly sorted and dusted, on the long shelf over the back door. The boxes reached to the ceiling, hundreds of boxes.

"Tom, I'm not sure that shelf . ."

An ominous screek. *Craaaaaack!* The wall of boxes crumbled, avalanching, tumbling, bouncing down all over them, spilling shoes, hats, gloves, corsets, mousetraps, mackinaws.

Dust settled over the quiet mound of boxes and higgledy-piggledy merchandise. Then a box stirred, rolled down the heap, and Mr. Springer's head appeared. "Tom? Tom? Tom, you all right?"

Mr. Springer clambered up, shedding boxes and merchandise, and began to search through the heap. After a while he came on Tom's shoe. "Tom? You there?"

Tom's voice came muffled from beneath a box of dish towels. "I think I'm dead, Mr. Springer. What'll my mother say?"

Wading through the boxes, Mr. Springer helped Tom up.

"Whew," said Tom, opening his eyes. "That was worse than the time I was loading hay bales on Mr. Meyer's truck."

"You've had accidents like this before?"

"My mother says I have too many ideas."

"Any ideas about cleaning up?"

"I always seem to have my ideas *before* things happen. Afterwards everything just gets confusing."

APPETIZERS

"By George," said Mr. Waley. "There they are, Jess."

"*Crocus Sieberi*," said Mr. Crofut lovingly.

Scamp barked.

"They'll look real pretty on Ma's breakfast table."

"Breakfast table?" Mr. Crofut straightened up. "You can't pick them, Henry."

"I promised Ma, Jess."

Scamp sniffed the crocuses.

"Henry, we agreed. When we started this here garden, we agreed: nothing's picked unless we both okay it."

"It's Martha, Jess. Just this morning she was drying her hands and gazing at the table. 'It'll be so nice,' she says, 'to have the first crocuses setting in a vase there in the sunlight.'"

"And then it'll be the first daffodils, Henry."

"Jess. It's *Martha*, not some stranger."

"Nope."

"Just one then, Jess, just one. She'll be happy with one. And you know we promised each other to compromise, you know it."

"Well," said Mr. Crofut. "I guess there's no harm in one."

But when they turned back to the flowerbed, instead of fat crocus sprouts, there were only lopped, raggedly chewed stalks.

"Cutworms?" cried Mr. Waley. "So fast?"

Scamp sighed behind them. They turned. He lay with his chin on his paws. The tip of a crocus leaf peeped from his jaws.

"I guess he figured if they was good enough to argue over, they'd be good enough to eat," said Mr. Waley.

"Well," said Mr. Crofut, "then we'd best spend an hour or two arguing over them weeds sprouting in the onions. Come on, Scamp. Dessert's over this way."

THE SCOLDING OR THE PIE

As Mr. Higgins was coming through the hill meadow with his grandson's dog, Dan, at his heels, he spied a kite struggling up out of the bramble thicket behind the saphouse.

"Now who'd be flying a kite today, Dan?" he said to the dog. "School's not out. Maybe someone's playing hooky."

He ducked under the barbed-wire fence and, stooping, entered the thicket, picking his way along where the brambles were thinnest. Dan scurried on ahead.

After a moment, around a corner, Mr. Higgins came on his grandson, Ben, with Dan beside him, both watching the kite dip and soar high overhead in the spring sunshine.

"Home from school early, Ben?"

"I never went. I got off the bus at Clarkson's. But I'm scared what Miss Fitzgerald's going to say tomorrow in school. Mom'll *never* give me an excuse. She'll say I have to take my medicine."

"Ben," said his grandfather, "you might just as well be back in that classroom if you're going to spend all day worrying. You're like a girl eating an ice cream cone in her best clothes: she's so busy catching drips, she can't taste the ice cream."

"Do you think grandmother will give me lunch?"

"Yes, and a scolding beside. She'll scold you all the time she's heaping the chicken and dumplings and white gravy on your plate and cutting you a second slice of apple pie. Now are you going to set your mind on the scolding or the pie?"

Ben grinned.

"Now if it was your grandmother's *mince* pie," said grandfather, sitting down on a rock in the meadow, "if it was her *mince*, why then you'd be wise to set your mind on the scolding. Her mince is terrible."

DOG DAYS

"Jack, dear, you played very nicely with Lucy Thompson this afternoon. I'm proud of you."

"Oh. Yeah," said Jack. "Could I have some more beans?"

His father looked up from the roast.

"Played with who?"

"Lucy Thompson. Zelda's little girl. He's been so wild lately, I didn't know what I'd do. Up on Mr. Sims' barn roof throwing crab-apples at the pigs below. Tormenting poor Mrs. Hoisington by painting her roses blue. Every time he goes out, you can hear him in West Shushan—the screen door banging, yelling 'Geronimo!' or 'Banzai!' at the top of his lungs as he leaps off the porch steps. More mashed potatoes, dear? But today he played all afternoon with Lucy. She's such a *nice* girl. Isn't she, Jack?"

"Oh. Yeah. If you like girls."

"They played house in the tent. It was the cutest thing."

Jack blushed, staring down into his mashed potatoes.

"Jack built a stove out of bricks and carried in wood and then they pretended to cook the fudge Lucy had brought with her. And then—George, it was the cutest thing, you really wouldn't have recognized your own son: Lucy pretended Tige was her baby and they wrapped him up in an old blanket and Jack rocked him in his arms..."

"Geez," muttered Jack.

"...and then they swang and swang under the apple tree, laughing and singing, Lucy's hair flying out in the sunshine."

"Well, Jack," said his father. "You young rapscallion."

"Aw," said Jack, "I only did it because Tige likes to swing. So Lucy said she'd hold him on. I mean, you know, I couldn't care less, I guess I'd rather break a leg than play with a girl, but Tige likes to swing."

MORE IDEAS

Mr. Springer and Tom had been cleaning the cellar of the General Store all morning. The work had gone slowly because every time Mr. Springer had gone upstairs to wait on a customer, Tom had stopped whatever he was doing—shoveling trash into a box, scrubbing a shelf—to try and figure out a quicker way of doing it.

Then late in the morning Mr. Springer came back downstairs to find Tom stuck under a cupboard. He moved some boxes and a chest of drawers and then shifted the cupboard so Tom could squirm out.

"I thought if I could carve a hole in the bottom and..." Tom's voice trailed off. "I guess maybe it wasn't such a good idea."

"Tom," said Mr. Springer. "I think *I've* just had an idea."

"I'm fired?"

"No, we're going fishing. A vacation might do us both good."

So Mr. Springer hung a sign on the door: *Gone on Business*, and they set off through the marsh to the river.

An hour later Mr. Springer's hat was bobbing along under Squire's bridge, and they were trudging back through the marsh. At every step Mr. Springer's shoes squelched. Tom hopped barefoot from tuft to tuft, his wet shoes tied around his neck. Mr. Springer paused to wring out his shirttail. Tom waited, combing mud out of his hair with his fingers.

They had fallen in, losing poles, bait box, and Mr. Springer's hat, when the riverbank collapsed under them.

"Tom," said Mr. Springer as they went on, "I've lost my keys, too. We'll have to ask Mrs. Griswold to lend us her set."

They tramped around onto Main Street. Waiting for Mrs. Griswold to get her keys, they contemplated their reflections in the window of Kaempfer's Insurance: as bedraggled and muddy as two muskrats.

"Well," said Tom at last, "at least it wasn't *my* idea to go fishing."

MOTHS!?!

One afternoon Mr. Burt came into the kitchen blowing on his hands and said there was snow in the air, he'd need his long underwear before long. So Mrs. Burt left off talking to the stewed tomatoes bubbling and spouting in the pot, and they went up to the attic.

Well. The kitchen door swinging shut behind them reminded Mrs. Burt of Aunt Maudie's house, where...She rattled on all the way up the stairs: why, just yesterday Mrs. Carpil had said...and so *she* had said...and Mrs. Carpil had come right back...And speaking of Mrs. Carpil put her in mind of Mrs. Sanders, poor soul, such a...

So Mr. Burt sat down on the attic stairs to catch his breath and wait for her to finish.

Up in the attic she was going on about her Grandma Hatty's old trunk and wondering where that brass candlestick had come from, and that old teapot, and handing Mr. Burt his long underwear...

"Moths," said Mr. Burt, holding up the suit of underwear.

"I don't hold with no moths now," Mrs. Burt rattled on. "Won't have them. Mrs. Carpil has them. Joe Curry said he saw them last week when he was fixing her roof."

"Moths!" said Mr. Burt again and shook his long underwear so the moths flew up in a cloud right in front of Mrs. Burt.

"Moths!?!" she screamed and went white as a sheet and got up off her knees and gawped. Mr. Burt said it was the only time in forty years he'd seen her speechless.

But after a minute she began to get a hold on herself and first she groaned and then a gargle came up her throat and then she nodded four or five times and blinked and said, "Hoo!" and then "Hum!" and then, all of a sudden, she was going again, "Well, I never. That Joe Curry must have brought those moths from Mrs. Carpil's in his toolbox. I declare. I never..."

ARGUMENTS

Jim and his father were always arguing. The first day out in the spring they'd argue over which way home plate was supposed to face. Jim's father would pull out his rule book and *show* Jim which way it was supposed to go. So Jim would say, Naw, he had the book turned upside down, or, Naw, that was only in the big leagues, it was different for kids. Some days they'd get so hot and deep into an argument the rest of the team would just lead them off to one side and practice without them.

During a game the team couldn't do that, of course. Jim's father was the coach. Jim didn't care. One day, right in the middle of a game, he yelled out, "Walk him? Dad, you're crazy!"

"Walk him, Jim!" shouted his father from the bench.

So Jim threw down his mask and began arguing with his father. And pretty soon Joe Fregosi, who's the first baseman, couldn't stand it anymore and told Jim his father was right, look, there were men on second and third. So Eddie Wilcox, the pitcher, told Joe he was acting stupid, look who was up next, and *they* began to argue, and pretty soon the whole team was shouting and yelling at each other all up and down the first-base line, and then Joe shoved Hank Cross, the shortstop, and somebody dared somebody else to punch him, and he did, and so the game was called on account of riot.

The next day the team talked it over and then went to see Mr. Florsheim, who's president of the league, and the next day Jim's father was appointed head league umpire.

So now when Jim and his father argue, it's legitimate, and after they've been at it a few minutes, the rest of the team crowds around Jim and whispers, "Don't, Jim. He'll throw you out. Leave it go." And then they shoulder between Jim and his father and finally pull Jim away and walk him up and down till he cools off.

MAIN COURSE

"Last one in's a rotten egg," said Mr. Waley, hurrying gingerly over the pebbles toward the riverbank. KERSPLUSH!

"Swan dive!" cried Mr. Crofut. KERSPLUSH!

"More like an old chicken," said Mr. Waley, bobbing in the current.

Scamp trotted off over the bridge, appearing a moment later wading through the gentle current under the bridge. Reaching the pool, he launched off across it, dog-paddling, head up, and was soon romping and barking with the children.

Then Mr. Crofut, diving again, spluttered up glancing wild-eyed about. "Henry," he whispered. "Henry."

Scamp paddled by him, dove, reemerged, and shaking himself, waded off under the bridge. A moment later he appeared overhead on the bridge, something scarlet and dripping hanging from his mouth.

"Henry," whispered Mr. Crofut. "I've lost my trunks. That last dive."

Scamp barked. They both glanced up.

"Scamp's got them, Jess. Look."

Scamp barked and pawed the ground, asking to be chased.

"We'll have to have help," said Mr. Waley. "A general chase." He raised his voice: "Ladies and gentlemen."

The splashing died down. Everybody turned to look at him.

"My friend here, Mr. Jesse Crofut, whom I'm sure you all know, has just had the misfortune.."

Scamp barked. Mr. Crofut's scarlet swimming trunks plummeted through the sunlight SPLAT into the pool and sank slowly into the depths. Everyone laughed and returned to their splashing, swimming, chatting. Mr. Waley retrieved the trunks.

"Well," he said, "at least Scamp didn't eat them like the crocuses. You'd have been here till dusk."

"Midnight," said Mr. Crofut, shivering. "It's a full moon."

Norman Rockwell

HOMEWORK

"Jim," said his father, "you'll just have to leave me alone. I've got an important meeting tomorrow. I've got to get this work done."

"What am I doing? I just said you'd . . ."

"Mary?" called his father. "Mary?"

Jim's mother came in from the kitchen drying a platter.

"John, he's really being very quiet. Are you stuck?"

"Maybe it's like I was on my homework earlier," said Jim, "when I couldn't see why thirty-eight didn't go into 889 twenty-three point ninety-seven times, and you showed me?"

"It's not really the same thing, Jim," said his mother. "You run along outside now. Your father's work is more complicated."

"Yes, but, Mom, there's . . ."

"No buts," said his mother. "Out. And don't slam the door."

Jim stamped out.

"Is it terribly difficult, John?" she asked.

"I just can't seem to work the equation out. I know what I want to do, but I just can't do it."

Jim's voice came through the open window.

"It's because he's got two plus two equals three, right in the second column."

His father glanced down at his papers.

"Mary, he's right."

Jim climbed over the windowsill. "Wasn't I right?"

His mother laughed.

"Jim, I'm just going to have to ask Miss Jowett not to give you any more homework. You're not going to have time to do *your* homework every night and still help your father with *his*."

STOVEPIPE

"I don't believe it," said Tom's father.

"Oh, *no!*" said his mother.

His father tried to wriggle the stovepipe off Tom's head.

"Owwwwwwwwww. Mr. Springer already triiiied that, Pop."

"We'll have to cut it off. I'll get my tinsnips."

Tom's voice echoed hollowly out of the stovepipe: "I was being real careful, Mom, and Mr. Springer even kept telling me to be careful, not to have any ideas, because of what happened last week. And I was, I was being real careful, going real slow, just like you said. But all of a sudden, I don't know, maybe the bench slipped, it wasn't me anyway, and there was this awful crash, the cat squalling, my head bunging against something, Mr. Springer exclaiming, and the next thing I knew, Mom, everything had gone dark, pitch dark. So I thought I'd gone blind or something; everytime I moved my head, there was a loud *clank!* But then Mr. Springer knocked on the stovepipe and told me what had happened, and tried to work it off my head but he couldn't, so he gave Tim Wilson a quarter to lead me home."

His father sheared the stovepipe off Tom's head while Tom muttered, "Oo, take it easy, ouch, that's my ear, be careful, Pop, will you, ow . . . Hi, Mom, I'm out!"

His mother sighed.

"And, Mom, at first Mr. Springer said I was fired. 'I can't afford you, Tom,' he said. 'I can't. You're a nice boy, but I can't afford you.' I began to cry. It was so dark and sooty and lonesome in the stove pipe. So Mr. Springer said, well, all right; at least I hadn't been trying out some wild idea this time."

"Tom," said his mother. "Was it an idea?"

"Well, I did sort of think that maybe if I put one foot *against* the stove? But it wasn't a *real* idea, Mom, not like the ones I usually think up."

NOTHING TO DO BUT WAIT

There were all those daisies, of course. But what could you do with daisies? Well, you could pick your mother a handful if she'd caught you last night feeding Spot your liver under the tablecloth. Or you could play "She loves me, she loves me not." Hunh!

But what else was there? He and Spot had roughhoused till they'd both lain back in the grass, panting. They'd chased butterflies, rooted in a last-year's woodchuck burrow. He'd screech-whistled through pieces of grass till his grandfather had groaned in his sleep, "Billy."

So he'd shied rocks as far down the hill and then as high into the sky as he could, and peppered the rotten trunk of a dead maple across the road till his arm was sore.

Maybe his father had forgotten he was supposed to pick them up on his way back from Shushan. Probably he'd just stopped to see Mr. McHenry and got to talking.

He picked a daisy and idly plucked off the petals. He bit one. It didn't taste so bad: greenish. Yuch! He spat. It was bitter. He nibbled at the yellow center. Worse. Like a swamp.

He picked another daisy and smelled it. Wow! Daisies smelled like dogs!?! Naw. Spot had been sitting on that one. He picked another. No smell at all. She loves me, she loves me not.

Say! He could play a Red Sox's game with the daisies. He hit it, he hit it not. Sure! And if the last two petals were real close and came off together, it was a double; and if it was three, a triple; and if one *dropped* off . . .

By the time his father's pickup truck rattled onto the gravel shoulder, the Red Sox were leading the Orioles one to nothing in the bottom of the third, and he was so caught up he'd begun to cheat a little.

GRIZZLY

Sam had just snatched off Jack's cap and lit out, Jack whooping after him, when all of a sudden he pulled up short.

"Grizzly," he said. "I forgot Grizzly, Jack. My mole. He's back in my desk."

They snuck around the school and peeped in the window. Miss Thatcher was correcting papers at her desk.

"If we don't rescue him, he'll starve," said Sam.

"Yeah, but how? With her sitting at her desk?"

They sat down under the window to think.

"I got it!" said Jack. "Lucy. Miss Thatcher would never suspect her."

So they ran after Lucy, catching up with her by Howard's Store.

"All right, Jack," she said when he'd explained to her. "But it won't bite me, will it?"

Peeping through the window, Sam and Jack watched her enter the schoolroom and tell Miss Thatcher she'd forgotten her notebook and take it out of her desk and sidle between two desks so she could come back down the aisle Sam's desk was in. She paused beside it, glanced back at Miss Thatcher, lifted the top of the desk, reached in . . . She had it! *Squeeeeeek!* She'd scared him. Miss Thatcher looked up. Lucy turned pale. And then suddenly she began to cough and staggered toward the open window, her hand shot out, Grizzly plummeted into Sam's cupped hands. Sam and Jack scrambled around the corner of the schoolhouse, hearing Lucy behind them saying, "I had something in my throat, Miss Thatcher."

Later, after they'd left her at her gate and were sitting on Sam's front porch while he fed Grizzly, Jack said, "See? And you're always kidding me about her. She's okay."

"Well," said Sam, "for a girl anyway."

DESSERT

"We've finally gotten to Scamp's season," said Mr. Crofut, handing his shotgun to Mr. Waley and ducking under the fence. "No more eating crocuses or stealing swimsuits. Hunting season comes around, he's all business. Look at him."

Scamp was running back and forth ahead of them, his nose to the ground. Suddenly he froze and began to creep slowly toward a clump of sumac.

"There. He's set one," whispered Mr. Crofut. "Come on."

They cocked their guns and advanced cautiously through the dry yellow grass, until Mr. Waley tripped over a root and fell, his gun booming into the sky. The partridge whirred off through the sumac.

In an overgrown pasture beyond a woodlot Scamp pointed again. Mr. Crofut signed to Mr. Waley to watch his feet. But as Mr. Waley silently pushed aside the canes of an alder bush, one snapped back, switching across his cheek.

"Ech!"

The partridge whirred away; Mr. Crofut's shotgun banged futilely. Scamp trotted back and barked up at Mr. Waley.

In a field dotted with cedars Scamp pointed for the third time. Mr. Waley checked himself all over, clamped his pipe in his teeth; they edged through the dry grass. Closer and closer.

Crack!

The partridge whirred away, banking between the cedars. Mr. Waley threw his cap down and stamped on it.

"What was *that*?" asked Mr. Crofut. Scamp growled.

"My *pipe*," said Mr. Waley. "I bit it right off." He held up the nub end of his pipestem. "I was concentrating so hard."

"Watch out!" said Mr. Crofut. "Scamp's got your hat!"

Mr. Waley reached for his cap, then straightened up.

"Scamp," he said. "Chew away. I deserve it."

RABBITS AND MOLES IN THE TREES

"What you got to watch," said Billy's grandfather, "is the fire going underground."

"Fire can't go underground," said Billy. "What would it burn?"

"Roots," said his grandfather. "Trash people have buried. Ancient Indian burial chambers. Nuts, seeds, beetle carcasses."

"So what happened the time the fire went underground?"

"How'd you know it had?" asked his grandfather, grinning. "Well it don't matter. It did. George Sanders was burning leaves by an old tree stump and left it smouldering while he went to milk his cow. Three days later young Tom Sims come barreling out of his parents' house yelling there was a dragon in the kitchen sink. Of course, no one believed in dragons, so all our fathers edged into the Sims' kitchen armed with shotguns, pitchforks, and bowie knives. A tongue of flame was spurting out of the cold water faucet. Everybody went home and looked into their washing machines, down their wells. Flames everywhere. Smoke billowing out of toilets, cracks in cellar floors. You'd stick a newspaper down a woodchuck hole and draw it out blazing. 'So that's why all them moles and rabbits has been setting up in the trees the past few days', says Mr. Abrams."

"What'd you do?"

"What could we do? We had to smother it. Sent off for a carload of asbestos shingles and tar and electrical tape, and then on the appointed day we sealed the ground under East Pomfert: taped faucets, shingled and tarred toilets, wells, rabbit burrows. They gave us kids a penny for every worm hole we could find. You'd look out across a field and see nothing but kids crawling over it on their hands and knees, dragging pots of tar behind them."

"But it worked?"

"Some say yes, some no. Put your hand to the ground. Don't it feel warm? The fire may be smouldering yet. Who knows?"

WINTER'S AFTERNOON

She acted like she *owned* him! He'd been standing there at the top of Vaughn's Hill with the rest of the fellows, Bill and Joe and Sam and Ned—all talking at once about how they were going to make a train of sleds, everyone hanging onto the feet of the one in front . . . And right then Lucy had come over and said,

"Will you take me down now, Jack? Like you promised?"

Everybody had gone silent. And then Sam had said,

"Will you take me down now, Jack? Like you promised?"

So it was all up with Lucy. In spite of the chocolate cakes and *Mars Bars,* in spite of the bones for Tige. She acted like she owned him! Girls were all right till they started *bothering* someone . . . coming up to him when he was with Joe and Bill and Sam! . . .

Oh, she was sorry now. He could see that, the way she trailed along behind him on the snowy sidewalk, scuffling her shoes. But so what? Tomorrow she'd forget all over again.

In front of her house he turned and faced her.

"Oh, Jack," she said, looking up. "Wait. I'll get the earmuffs you lent me yesterday."

She ran inside. He waited grimly. She peeped out around the front door, smiling expectantly.

"Well?" he growled.

And just then the warm lovely smell of new baked chocolate cake reached him, stamping his feet there in the snow under the gray winter's sunset.

"Jack, my mother just baked. And there's cocoa."

He kicked the gatepost and started up the walk. He'd throw her over tomorrow. He sniffed. Her mother must have baked gingerbread, too. Well . . . Next Thursday at the latest.

MISS FOSTER'S CHRISTMAS PRESENT

 The third night of the Christmas pageant hardly anyone was out in the audience—a few parents and grandparents, a teacher or two. Billy Hoisington, playing King Herod, lounging back on a sofa with pillows stuffed under his toga, had just ordered his army to pursue the Holy Family, who at that very moment were fleeing into Egypt across the other side of the stage.

So Tom Murphy, who was playing a General, bawled out, "Ready! HARCH!" and banged the end of his spear down on the stage. And just then, out of the corner of his eye, he saw a dog grab the class's Christmas present for Miss Foster off a table in the wings.

So he dropped his spear and lit out after the dog, piling into the rest of the Roman Army, which was just executing a right-left countermarch to get in line behind him and tramp off in pursuit of the Holy Family. Everyone went down in a clatter of spears and tin helmets. Tom clambered up, the others yelling and pushing at him, caught a glimpse of the dog galloping out the side door, and then was pulled under again, and yelled and thrashed and hit out and finally left the whole Roman Army in a heap behind him on the stage, the audience roaring with laughter.

Running by the dark glee club room, he yelled at Joe Bentley (who was in there pretesting the Christmas party refreshments) to come on, a dog had stolen Miss Foster's present.

Joe caught up with him halfway across the parking lot.

"Where's it headed?"

"Main Street."

They skidded around the corner onto Main Street. Up ahead they could see the dog trotting in and out of the crowds of kids and last-minute shoppers on the sidewalk, the package dangling from his mouth.

"Forward!" yelled Tom, throwing back his cloak. Joe, one of the Three Kings, gathered up the skirts of his robes, and they charged up the sidewalk. Children scattered before them. A lady struck out at them with her pocketbook.

At Tom's yell the dog glanced behind him and then veered off down the alley by Kaempfer's Insurance. Tom skidded around two little girls and flung after him. Joe stumbled, skidded, arms flailing, and tumbled into a snowdrift.

"Take the front," Tom yelled. The alley was a dead end. He slid to a stop by the back door of Springer's General Store. It was ajar. He peered in: a dimly lit backroom, piles of boxes, silent, deserted. He crept warily up an aisle between piles of boxes.

"RRROWF!"

The dog started up out of the shadow under Mr. Springer's old rolltop desk and galloped into the front of the store, ears flapping, the package still dangling from his mouth.

"No dogs allowed, Tom Murphy, you know that!" cried Mr. Springer as Tom dashed after the dog through the checkout counter and past Mrs. Bruce, who had just opened the front door. There was a shout, and Tom slid to a stop on the sidewalk beside Joe, sprawled in the snowbank clutching a scrap of Christmas wrapping paper.

"I got part of it!" he yelled, scrambling up. They tore after the dog.

Beyond the bank, the dog suddenly turned and, galumphing through the snowdrifts, laboring up the steps, gained the porch of the summer hotel. He galloped down the porch and then, as Mr. Sears, the watchman, opened the door to see what was going on, darted through his legs and into the hotel.

Tom and Joe dashed up the steps. Mr. Sears was picking himself up, looking around for his flashlight. Tom and Joe explained breathlessly what had happened.

"And there's everything we bought for Miss Foster in it," finished up Joe. "A scarf and handkerchiefs and candy."

Mr. Sears picked up his flashlight, brushed the snow off it, snapped it on and off. Then he looked down at Tom and Joe.

"It'll be known as The Great Mad Dog Hunt of 1970," he said. "Come in. If there's candy in that package, we haven't any time to lose."

Joe started in, but Tom hung back.

"Do you really think it's a *mad* dog, Mr. Sears?"

"Naw," said Joe over his shoulder. "It's Scamp. Mr. Crofut's dog. I recognized him when he bowled me over in front of Springer's."

In the lobby of the hotel all the chairs and tables were covered with dim white cloths. A streetlight glittered in the yellow glass eye of a moosehead.

"Listen for him now."

From far up the stairway they heard the faint thud of galloping feet. They crept up single file, hugging the wall: listening on the second floor...then on the third...then crawling out onto the fourth floor on hands and knees.

"I hear him," whispered Joe.

From far down the hall came the sound of ripping paper. The long hall was dark except for an occasional shaft of light from a streetlight.

"Take off your shoes," whispered Mr. Sears.

They snuck in their socks down the hall. The sound of chewing grew louder and louder until they stood outside the door of the last room.

"We'll rush him," whispered Mr. Sears. "Grab for the package."

The sound of chewing had stopped.

"On him!" yelled Mr. Sears.

"Geronimo!" shouted Tom.

"Remember the Maine!" yelled Joe.

In the sudden glare of the flashlight, they charged into the room. Joe dove for the candy, Tom for the box of handkerchiefs, Mr. Sears waving his arms and whooping behind them. Scamp, lying in the middle of the floor chewing the corner of a box, lunged through Mr. Sears' legs and fled down the hall, his nails clickety-clacking on the floorboards.

Tom and Joe carried Miss Foster's Christmas present back down Main Street, grinning proudly. People stopped to ask what had happened; little kids stared open-mouthed.

Back at school, everyone was crowded in the glee club room, talking excitedly about Tom's trampling exit over the prostrate Roman Army. Tom and Joe pushed through the crowd and spread the presents out in triumph before Miss Foster. A babble of voices. Tom and Joe climbed on the table. Cheers. They sketched their heroic chase through the wintry twilight. Redoubled cheers.

Outside Scamp barked.

"Couldn't we let him in, Miss Foster?" asked Tom. "It's Christmas."

So the door was opened, and Scamp squirmed in on his belly, casting contrite glances up at the Roman soldiers, and the front and back ends of camels and donkeys, the kings and shepherds and floppy winged angels jamming the glee club room. And then he was given a plate of vanilla ice cream and Christmas cookies, which he lapped at eagerly while Miss Foster opened her presents, exclaiming.